# Dear Parent:
## Your child's love of reading starts here!

Every child learns to read in a different way and at his or her own speed. Some go back and forth between reading levels and read favorite books again and again. Others read through each level in order. You can help your young reader improve and become more confident by encouraging his or her own interests and abilities. From books your child reads with you to the first books he or she reads alone, there are I Can Read Books for every stage of reading:

### SHARED READING
Basic language, word repetition, and whimsical illustrations, ideal for sharing with your emergent reader

### BEGINNING READING
Short sentences, familiar words, and simple concepts for children eager to read on their own

### READING WITH HELP
Engaging stories, longer sentences, and language play for developing readers

### READING ALONE
Complex plots, challenging vocabulary, and high-interest topics for the independent reader

### ADVANCED READING
Short paragraphs, chapters, and exciting themes for the perfect bridge to chapter books

I Can Read Books have introduced children to the joy of reading since 1957. Featuring award-winning authors and illustrators and a fabulous cast of beloved characters, I Can Read Books set the standard for beginning readers.

A lifetime of discovery begins with the magical words "I Can Read!"

*Visit www.icanread.com for information*
*on enriching your child's reading experience.*

# Bathtime for Biscuit

story by ALYSSA SATIN CAPUCILLI
pictures by PAT SCHORIES

HarperCollins*Publishers*

Library of Congress Cataloging-in-Publication Data

Capucilli, Alyssa.
　　Bathtime for Biscuit / story by Alyssa Satin Capucilli ; pictures by Pat Schories.
　　　　p.　cm.—(A my first I can read book)
　　Summary: Biscuit the puppy runs away from his bath with his puppy friend Puddles.
　　ISBN-10: 0-06-027937-0 (trade bdg.) — ISBN-13: 978-0-06-027937-0 (trade bdg.)
　　ISBN-10: 0-06-027938-9 (lib. bdg.) — ISBN-13: 978-0-06-027938-7 (lib. bdg.)
　　ISBN-10: 0-06-444264-0 (pbk.) — ISBN-13: 978-0-06-444264-0 (pbk.)
　　　[1. Dogs—Fiction. 2. Baths—Fiction.] I. Schories, Pat, ill. II. Title. III. Series.
PZ7.C179Bat 1998　　　　　　　　　　　　　　　　　　　　　　　　　　　　　97-49663
[E]—dc21　　　　　　　　　　　　　　　　　　　　　　　　　　　　　　　　　CIP
　　　　　　　　　　　　　　　　　　　　　　　　　　　　　　　　　　　　　　AC

❖

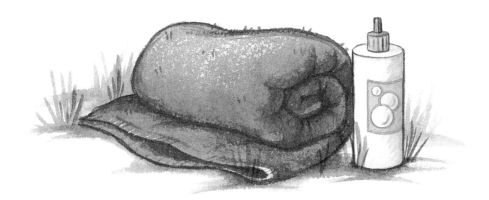

Time for a bath, Biscuit!

Woof, woof!

Biscuit wants to play.

Time for a bath, Biscuit!

Woof, woof!

Biscuit wants to dig.

Time for a bath, Biscuit!

Woof, woof!

Biscuit wants to roll.

Time for a bath, Biscuit!

Time to get nice and clean.

Woof, woof!

In you go!

Woof!

Biscuit does not want a bath!

Bow wow!
Biscuit sees
his friend Puddles.

Woof, woof!

Biscuit wants to climb out.

Come back, Biscuit!

Woof!

Come back, Puddles!

Bow wow!

Biscuit and Puddles
want to play
in the sprinkler.

Biscuit and Puddles
want to dig
in the mud.

Biscuit and Puddles
want to roll
in the flower bed.

Now I have you!

Woof, woof!

Let go of the towel,

Biscuit!

Bow wow!

Let go of the towel,

Puddles!

Silly puppies!

Let go!

Woof, woof!

Bow wow!

Oh!

Time for a bath, Biscuit!

Woof, woof!

A bath for all of us!